THE CUBE

Speak N.O.w or Forever Hold Your Peace

DONIELLE INGERSOL

CONTENTS

CHAPTER ONE

It is hard to say who the first person to enter the cube was. No one even knew where it had originated from. Perhaps there was some lab a hundred or so stories underground that came up with it. The substance that formed its interior was unlike anything anyone had ever seen before. I know, you might be saying to yourself that the old quote from an ancient book must be true, "There is nothing new under the sun." But the cube was new, definitely; and it was now under the sun. Someone released it one day or perhaps one night when the moon was full and round, and the coyote pack was howling as they looked into that silver orb. An occasional owl hooted in time with their chorus then everything suddenly became deathly still. Yes, I am going to say it came one midnight in October. The year? What year was it? OR, what year will it be? Are you ready for hell or will the CUBE be humanities new heaven? Again, the ancient book states that a new heaven and a new earth are coming, does it not?

My grandfather was out checking on some of the cattle when the CUBE arrived. Word came over his old radio that a terrible, north-easterner was coming. He had nearly a hundred head of cattle scattered over a thousand acres. If the CUBE had arrived back a little earlier, he would have been riding a horse, but he was not. He was on an ATV that had very heavy, duty shocks. He had rounded up half of the cattle with the help of Sheba, and Shank, his two border collies. They would bring them into a pen by Jake. He was at the gate waiting. Granddad figured the rest of the herd must be over the hill down by the stream that wound through a quarter of the ranch. It was protected there from the wind. There is something about cattle that can sense a storm. I always knew those big noses of theirs were good for something other than being all slimy, wet, and sticky. Maybe they used them to not only to smell out the sweetest grass but sense an upcoming storm also? Pops had stuck to the trail for two thirds of the way then turned off between two large boulders. He never made it through them. We found him there about 2 am.

There was this square thing. That is how I can best describe it. Well, maybe a CUBE would be a better term. When we got to the CUBE, he was inside of it stark naked. We could see him floating around inside as if in space. Sometimes he would be upside down and other times right side up. All of us took turns trying to break him out of his prison but to no avail. The exterior of that CUBE was harder than diamond, I swear. Nothing we tried could even scratch it.

Meanwhile, a hundred or so miles away, Kathy had been out for an evening walk. She often did this. It did not matter what season it was. She would dress for the weather. This evening however, she had not. She was wearing a light jacket and some black pants with orange designs in them. One minute the temperature had been tolerable and the next, a bitter cold wind had come and chilled her to the bones. Her teeth started rattling as she turned around and started for home. She also never made it. Her body iced over and a CUBE, the same size as the one that surrounded my grandfather formed around her. Her daughter found her inside the next morning stark naked, floating in some type of suspended animation. She called 911 and soon a fire truck arrived. They also tried everything they could to break her out, but to no avail.

The CUBES were only in these designated spots for 24 hours. After that length of time, they vanished along with their occupants. I say occupants because that first night hundreds of people had been CUBED all over the world. Twenty-four hours later they all vanished. You could walk through the place where the CUBE had been. Everything was as it was before, except sometimes a pile of clothes was found not far from the spot, all neatly folded as if the same person had been responsible for all the disappearances. There was something else strange about the clothes. Granddad had a pair of blue jeans he dearly loved. Grandmother had put patches on patches. Perhaps that was what he liked about them for Grandma had gone to her rest two years earlier. Perhaps the patches reminded him of her somehow. I do not know. When we found Granddad's jeans, they were perfectly folded and brand new. There was not a patch on them, and his old boots looked like they had just been purchased from the department store. There was not even a scuff on the toes and the heals looked like they had never set foot on a jagged rock. The next set of cubes did not arrive until exactly thirty-eight days later, this time instead of a thousand or so, a million or more people were CUBED.

Joe Marlo found the cattle exactly where he has suspected. They were huddled together under the group of giant Ponderosa Pine. Behind the pine there were some Douglas Fir that had sprung up over the last fourteen years. That was the year the great fire had swept over the ranch. Only the largest trees survived. This area was a great shelter from the wind, but it would not spare the cattle if temperatures plunged into the minus twenties. The younger cows would have a harder time surviving than those over two years old. It would be best to round them up and get them back to the corral. There was an open structure banked with large bales of hay. The cattle would be out of the wind and by huddling together under the overhanging roof could survive quite nicely, plus if five or more feet of snow came in it would not cause them to get stranded by themselves in some six-foot drift. He whistled for the two dogs. They arrived in about two minutes. In no time they had the beasts moving in the right direction, nipping at their heals if they tried to turn to the left or to the right. Back in the corral he counted heads. An old heifer and her calf were all that were missing. Joe knew if they were not found they would probably die so he decided to go back. This time he took a horse. This would give him the advantage of being higher up making it easier to spot the animals if they were laying down somewhere. Two hours later he found them. With the help of Sheba and Shank again he soon had them headed home. It had been a strenuous trip to get them all back. He was sixty-nine and not as young as he used to be.

Back at the house Grandma had a pot of hot, chicken soup boiling. She dipped him out a large bowl. Then as he was eating, Tim came into the room. It had been eight years since granddad had seen his son Tim. One day while he was out riding on the ranch his horse threw a shoe and he toppled off, hitting his head on a rock. It was a terrible loss to the family. Tim was 12, or so Dad thought and just old enough to help with the unending work that goes with ranching. Joe looked at his son. Something seemed wrong. Tim was still young. He came and sat down, and Mom also filled up a bowl of soup for him. He opened a package of crackers and crunched them up in the bowl before he spoke.

"So, dad, do you think this north-easterner is going to be as bad as they are saying, do you think it could dump 6' of snow out there? I have never seen that much snow except up in the mountains." Joe thought about the question between two or three slurps of soup before answering.

"I believe it will be as bad as they are saying, son. When I was out there between those two large boulders-the ones we call the pillars-a blast of cold air hit me the likes of which I had never felt before in all of my sixty-nine years."

"What do you mean, dad? You are not 69, you are only 61. What happened to you out there? When you came back, there were like another dozen wrinkles on your face. Now you are saying that you are 69? I am almost believing you. What happened in the last eight years that I might not know about?"

"For one, son. We have two new border collies, Sheba, and Shank. They are the best cow hands I ever had. Where it used to take three of us to round up them doggies, I can do it with the collies just as quick or quicker. Besides, since Junior ran off with that city gal, we are short-handed around here. There is only you, Bobby and Janice, your sister. You have a seven-year-old nephew. Did you know that?"

No, Dad, can't say as I do. What is his name?" Granddad scratched his head a couple of times as if trying to recall his name. He managed to get another couple of spoonsful of soup down before answering.

"His name is Russie. I expect when he gets a little bit older, he will go by Russel or Russ but for now he is Russie. By the way how old will you be this year when your birthday arrives?

"I will be 14, why do you ask?" Joe appeared relieved, like a great burden had been lifted from his tortured soul when he heard the news. His son was not only alive but a year older, maybe two. He had survived the fall. But then he knew that didn't he? Something got messed up back there by the pillars, something strange.

When Kathy got home, she went out to the wood pile and brought in three chunks of birchwood. She took a small hatchet and made up some kindling with one. Soon she had a blazing, hot fire going. Sandra came in with her boyfriend and settled down next to him in the love seat. He had brought his guitar. Paul had a great voice. He sounded as good as a lot of those country singers out there, even better than probably half of them. He wrote his own songs too. Tonight, he started singing his latest as the sparks made their way up the chimney. The tired mother sat down and listened. He called the song: *"Living on Love and Memories."* Kathy wondered as she listened if her daughter was pregnant, and he was trying to break the news to her in a way she could not get mad at them. John, Sandra's dad had run off with his secretary, Amy one weekend to Vegas and never returned. His daughter was now seventeen, so a check came in every month for child support. It was enough to pay the bills and mortgage payments. Mom did some housecleaning for about five people. That helped. The Smith's had asked her if she could sit their house for a week while they went on a trip to Hawaii. She had agreed.

LIVING ON LOVE AND MEMORIES

*We came together young
when life was tender
We played the games
that children always play
The country lanes and
hillsides were our haven
Soon the morning of
our lives turned into day*

*This thing called love grew
stronger with each moment
It set a time clockmovingin our souls
We couldn't feel the
heat of the noontime
Pressing slowly in upon
our simple goals*

*And now were living
on love and memories
Little Lesa's in her arms
We're struggling to keep
the wolf back from the door
Living on love and memories,*

her welfare check and mine
Dreaming the dreams,
we used to live before

One sunny day her
father came to see me
He pulled a shotgun
slowly from his side
He said, "Come on now
Son you're getting married
Soon I stood before
the alter with my bride

Yes, now were living on
love and memories
Little Lisa's in her arms
Funny how we thought
we'd have much more
Living on love and memories,
her welfare check and mine
Dreaming the dreams,
we used to live before
Dreaming the dreams,
we used to dream before
Dreaming the dreams,
we used to live before

The music drowned Kathy to sleep. She was not awake when John came over and picked her up in his huge arms then took her to the bedroom and tucked her under the covers. He sat there in his favorite chair as he watched her dream. From the other room he had listened to Paul strum out another country song. It really was uncanny how the song seemed to match the mood he was feeling. It had been so long since he had held Kathy in his arms like that. Did she even know that he loved her like no other woman he had ever met? He thought of the upcoming wedding where his little girl would stand before the alter with the very guy that was singing. When he found out she was pregnant, he demanded it. Paul started in on another original.

LOVE YOU WHILE YOUR SLEEPING

The clock ticks out the nighttime,
soon I know that it's the right time
For your breathing tells me that
you've gone to sleep
So I snuggle closer to you,
and I wrap my arms around you
Then I place a kiss gently on your
cheek

So, I love you while your sleeping
But I can't keep from weeping

When I know the love, I'm keeping
Must be kept for sleeping you
But I keep on a hoping
That your sleeping arms will open
And we'll love again as
lovers can and do

The o'l clock strikes three and
you roll over in your sleep
Then you mumble something,
can't quite make it out
But I pretend you said,
"I love you,' so I turn and say
"I love you too"
But only a fool would
ever make that out

So, I love you while your sleeping
But I can't keep from weeping
when I know the love, I'm keeping
Must be kept for sleeping you
But I keep on a hoping
That your sleeping arms will open
And we'll love again as
lover can and do
The chimes ring out the hours
But I don't seem to have the power
Or what it takes to take my arms away
from you
For soon you will awaken

And these arms will be forsaken
And who knows but what you'll find
somebody new.

So, I love you while your sleeping
But I can't keep from weeping
When I know the love, I'm keeping
Must be kept for sleeping you
But I keep on a hoping
That your sleeping arms will open
And we'll love again a
lovers can and do

The music stopped and John got up to see what was going on. Paul had left. Before exiting the home, he had pulled a knitted blanket from the wicker basket next to the fireplace and wrapped his girl in it. Sandra was sleeping soundly. She had a large teddy bear in her arms and a sweet smile on her face as if her dreams, where-ever they were, were wonderful and sweet. Perhaps Paul really did love her and was not marrying her because of the shotgun incident that had taken place. He was a clever lad. He had even written a song about it. You see, John was a strict Baptist and if a guy was going to go all the way with a gal, then this deacon was going to make certain he went all the way to the alter. And so, he had. But as he saw her there sleeping so contentedly, something deep down inside let him know everything was going to be alright with them. They would marry and stay together until death knocked on the door of one of them or the other. Now if only Kathy would wake up from her animated life, they too could be fully united again and grow old together. Somehow, she had gotten the idea he had run off with Amy. Where that had come from, he could never figure out.

CHAPTER TWO

The third wave of CUBE-ings came exactly thirty-eight days after the second wave. In this round, millions upon millions of people were CUBED. Everyone over the age of sixty was encased in these strange cubes. Richard was operating an excavator when the phenomena occurred. His business partner was suddenly taken into one of these square boxes. He raised the front of the machine and brought it down with great force on the top of the CUBE hoping to break it open. Don was inside floating around. When the force of the blow hit the top of the CUBE, his head slammed his head into the ceiling and blood came out. Don slumped down to the bottom of his cell and appeared to die right in front of those watching. From this they came to understand that some type of liquid was inside these indestructible CUBES. Shortly after Don appeared to die, the blood dissipated and the wound on his head healed. The process took only five minutes. During that time, Richard started to dig around the edges of the CUBE. He found that it was not a cube at all but the top of a rectangular structure that appeared to go down into the earth for who knew how deep? Where the first two phases of the CUBES occurred outside, this phase included people who were inside of buildings.

The President of the United States was CUBED along with several members of the house and senate. He was in the Lincoln Room when it happened. His wife not being sixty yet was not encased. There was trouble with China brewing. In fact, he was on the phone with its emperor when it happened. The leader of China also succumbed to the CUBE. It was funny how the subject matter they were talking about changed.

"President, what is your take on all our people being encased in CUBES and then dropping as it were off the face of the earth, never to be heard from again?" The president pondered the question for a moment. The satellite phone he was using could not be traced by any of the normal means. Technicians had installed an antenna on top of the White House to boost the signal so he could talk from anywhere in the building. He passed through the door into the hallway, looking for any personal that might be around, seeing none, he responded.

"I am not so sure they have dropped off the face of the earth. I believe they are still active, doing whatever they were doing before they were encased. Our economy has not suffered so what does that tell you? The wheels of commerce are still operating. The banks have not closed even though thousands of the C.O.s have gone missing. When a crime starts to happen, the person committing it is instantly enclosed in a CUBE so that the crime never takes place. Is that happening in China, also? Are you finding that crime is down?"

"Unlike the US, we do not have as much crime in our country even though our population is several times that of the United States. We have pretty much eliminated crime. Our people do not have guns as a whole and most crimes in your country are committed with guns, isn't that correct?" Again, the President pondered the question then answered.

"There are several guns for each American Citizen in our country but at this moment, we have far less crimes with guns. When the criminal is about to shoot their victim, the CUBE immediately freezes them in place. Their clothes are removed and left folded outside. And the weapon is also outside. That is what we do not understand. The weapon-and it need not be a gun-is there with their clothes. But it is useless. It has been transformed into the material that encases the criminal. Each one we have examined have not a single moving part. The material is so hard, nothing we have tried so far can destroy it. I expect if we came to the point in our countries where we-God forbid-decided to unleash our nuclear bombs against one another, that any people in CUBES would survive. Granted they would get shook up a bit, but we have not seen any person stay dead if they are in a CUBE. Blood may come out of some wounds they receive as they are bounced around and they might die for a couple of minutes, but life is restored, and the blood just disappears. It is the strangest phenomena we have ever witnessed. I also expect if we did come to the point of bombing each other with any of our weapons, they also would be rendered useless like those guns we find. What experience have you had along these lines with your citizens?" The Chinese leader did not answer right away. He could see someone trying to talk with him, it was as if they were right in front of him moving their lips, but he could not hear a word. Finally, he answered.

"I am sorry, Mr. President but an urgent matter has come up that demands my immediate attention. Perhaps we can continue this conversation later." With that he was gone, and the President looked around. At least in the White House everything appeared to be normal. The CUBES this time around were only visible for ten minutes. Something was speeding up the process. This CUBE system was gaining in intelligence. It was like some prophet that could see into the future before it happened, and nothing could stop the events ordained from taking place.

Back at the ranch, since Grandpa and Grandpa were gone now, Junior and his wife had moved back. There were only the three kids now and Jake, and me of course. I was there witnessing everything that was taking place. From a kid's standpoint, it was quite strange. I had been five when Grandma died. Some type of cancer had taken her. I saw Grandpa crying for the first time in my life. His weathered old face was moist with tears, great sobs were coming from somewhere down deep inside his body. She had been by his side for forty-eight years and now she was gone. His eyes that used to be so sparkly and clear were now clouded over. The spark was gone out of them. He limped also when he walked and that head, he used to hold up so high was bowed down most of the time. I liked the dogs. And Jake had always taken a likening to me. But two years had passed. I was older. Jake was teaching me how to drive the ATV. I loved feeling the dry wind in my face as we raced over the fields. He showed me how to look way ahead and avoid hitting the rocks that lay around on top of the ground or in some cases appeared to rise out of the earth. It was while on one of these trips I witnessed the first animal CUBED. There was a prize bull that Grandpa loved. He had fathered a lot of calves and everyone of them might have been a county fair winner in the right hands.

We had just passed through the pillars where they said Granddad had been taken when up ahead, a CUBE rose out of the ground and encased that bull. Jake had seen one person CUBED and so knew the size of them. This one was at least twice as large. He stopped driving and we went over to get a closer look. At first the animal inside looked like he was going through a car wash. Powerful streams of some liquid scrubbed him clean. The dirt and grime all over his body was on the outside in a pile. His eyes had opened large as saucers when the Jetstream had pulverized him. If he complained, we could not hear him. Once the structure of the CUBE was in place, he fixed his eyes on Jake as if begging for help. His mouth opened and it looked like he was saying "help me, get me out of here, quick." But then who can read a cow's lips? Can you? Five minutes later he was gone and a dozen prize heifers with him. Jake just shook his head.

"What do you think of that, Russie?" I was of course intrigued by it all. For me it had been fascinating. There was this force that was as strong or stronger than the high winds that often rolled across the ranch. I remembered that once I was nearly blown off my feet by a gust of wind. Had a fence post not stopped me, I might have been whisked away. I did not like the electric shock I received though. No cow should be subject to that kind of treatment.

"I don't know, J," I responded. I called him J, short for Jake. "I think it was awesome, just awesome! Do you think all of the cattle will be CUBED?"

"No, son, only the older ones but not too old. If they are too old that thing probably will not touch them. It looks like it is only taking the best of the herd, leaving the older ones that will be going to market and the younger ones that need to put a lot of meat on their bones yet." We headed back to the ranch to tell the family what had happened. It was a sober lot that evaluated the losses later that day. No less than fifty head of cattle had simply disappeared. We decided to round up the ones going to market the very next week and get some money in the bank. This might be a long ordeal so preparations needed to be made to weather the storm that probably would be far worse than any Northeasterner.

After the chosen cattle had been taken to the market, the remaining Marlo gang decided to take a trip into town to get some things that would sustain us over the winter. On the way we saw a lot of CUBING going on. It was not so much people this time but the animals and birds that were captured and removed from the face of the planet. I watched a long rectangle spiral come out of the ground and encase a bird in mid-flight. It was followed by half a dozen others. A rabbit ran across the road in front of our vehicle and was CUBED in the air as it jumped over the ditch. The CUBES did not last more than a few seconds now. They would appear and be gone.

In town we were surprised at how few people were shopping. There was no one in sight over sixty years old. There was also no age limit to who could work now. Kids worked right along with their parents. They helped to fill the vacant places of the missing in action. I wanted a bicycle for Christmas. Mom and Dad promised to get one for me. I got to pick it out even. At Walmart I found the one I wanted. It had big tires so going over the rough ground at the ranch would not be so bad. If I hit a rock, it would not be felt so much as the larger tire would absorb some of the shock. It was then they told me another little sister was on the way. I had one already and she was a pain to deal with. What would I do with two of them running around bugging me? Why couldn't I get a brother anyway? On the way home there was not a single animal CUBED. Had the great machine gone silent for good?

Meanwhile in a CUBICLE of time the Marlo family were preparing for the best Christmas ever. Junior, his wife, Karen, Russie and little Katie were going to be there from the city and there was a rumor going around that she was pregnant with another girl. Jake was going to bring a gal he met up with in town over for Christmas to introduce her to the family. Wedding bells were coming up. Bobbie, the middle son was going to be bringing his new girlfriend over also for Christmas dinner. He had been dating her for six months and it appeared they were going to tie the knot. Yes, it would be a great Christmas. Everyone was going to be home, the entire family together again. Well, probably not Christel. She had gotten polio at the age of

7 and as the condition worsened, it came to the point where she could do nothing for herself. She had to be waited on hand and foot. So, her aunt, who had a home for special needs people, had taken her in. Christel would not be there. Grandmother addressed Jake as she put the finishing touches on a giant pumpkin pie she was making.

"Have you killed and plucked the turkey, Jake? I need to start stuffing it, getting it ready for the oven." The farm hand scratched his ear as he listened. A little flake of ear wax had exited the canal and he flicked it away from his finger.

"I will go and do it right away, Mum." Though not a member of the family he called her that. It was as close to Mom as he could personally go. His mother had walked out on him at a young age. He never heard from her again. When nobody showed up to claim him, grandma took him in. He had been there ever since. His dad had gone off to war leaving his wife to raise him. She just didn't want to bother. Dad was listed missing in action. That was ages ago it seemed. Out at the pen he looked at the grand bird. It was a shame to have to kill him. Then a thought occurred to him. The co-op down town had just gotten in a few butterballs. A plan formed in his mind. Leaving the ranch from a back road he took his truck in and selected the biggest fattest one he could find. Three quarters of an hour passed before he delivered the unwrapped bird to the waiting cook. She hardly gave it notice as a van had pulled up sometime while he was gone. Christel had come home. She was still in a wheelchair but had all her muscles working except for one weak ankle. She looked amazing. Aunt Rachel was beaming. It had been a miraculous six months. One day the young lady was bedridden, the next she was alert and sitting up in bed. After undergoing therapy, tremendous progress had occurred. They told her in another month she would fully recover from any remaining effects of that debilitating disease. She told her aunt she wanted to come home and probably stay for good. So, two more plates would need to be set at the giant oak table.

Grandfather and Junior had gone down to the stream at the north end of the ranch and cut a beautiful Douglas Fir for a Christmas tree. Four people were even now going through the assortment of ornaments and decorating it. Even before they were finished, packages of all shapes and sizes, wrapped in sparkling paper were appearing under the tree. Tim was hoping for an ATV of his very own. Russie of course had been bugging his parents for a bike. Grandmother had purchased a make-up kit with perfume for Rosalie but since she would not be here, she wrapped it up for Christel. Her sister would have to settle for some spices and a candle. But more surprises were yet to come. About that time a large Cadillac pulled up into the driveway and an elderly couple got out and made their way to the door. Jake recognized his mother immediately and was that his dad? He couldn't believe it! It was. It was. After all these years he was alive. He ran toward the tall man with his arms spread open. It took only a few seconds for the elderly gentleman to realize this was his son, all grown up. And to think he was getting married?

The world of the CUBE was a wonderful world indeed for those who had been captured and whisked off to what appeared to be paradise. Wars did not exist in this realm. Crime was a thing of the past. People seldom died. Those who entered sick were mysteriously healed of their diseases. Friends and family long separated were united again. There was prosperity in this land of the blessed or so they appeared to be blessed. Thousands of questions that had plagued people about what had happened were answered. It was good, almost too good to be true, and perhaps that is the truth of it all were the truth even available to be known.

CHAPTER THREE

When Paul got back to his house, both of his parents were gone. After inquiring about them from a neighbor they told him they had been encapsuled and after a few minutes had disappeared with all the others that had been grabbed. It was sad. It was hard enough to see how his girlfriend suffered from the loss of her mom and dad let alone the other problems that family had. As he thought of his parents, a deep longing came over him to see them again. Why had he not spent more time with them while they were around? He wondered if he would ever see them again. What would happen to his father's business? Tomorrow he would need to do what he had failed to do, go there and work. He would probably have to take the business over. These hard times called for hard choices. Right now though, bed was in order. As he dropped off to sleep, he thought of his girl. He would be a father soon to a child who would never know her grandmothers or grandfathers.

The next day at the shop the crew welcomed him to the team and told him they hoped he would keep the business going. They needed the work and there was a steady stream of clients coming for tires.

"You do not have to worry, guys. We will keep going as long as we can. If you are willing, Bill to fill me in on the details of how to run this business, I will try my best to not disappoint everybody. Together we must do this, make it happen. Besides I have a daughter coming in a few months and we will need to pay the bills." Bill got a strange look on his face as he heard the news. So, Paul's girl was pregnant. It seemed like yesterday she was a little girl going to school. Now she must be all grown up.

"I've got your back, Paul." Bill lied. "If you are ready to give this a go then let's go." After work that day as he was thinking about his parents another song came to mind. He was saddened by his sudden loss so this would be a sad song. He sat down with his guitar and put it together.

KEEP IN TOUCH

I lived and grew as most boys
getting older every year
Until the army called me
to serve for her
As I stepped on that bus,
I heard my mother say
Keep in touch as she brushed
the tears away

Keep in touch, keep in touch
That's what we always say
when we part to go
our individual ways
keep in touch, keep in touch
please write or give me a ring
to let me know how things
are going your way

As a father loves his daughter
so did I love mine
It was our joy to watch her
grow in every way
At sixteen years she married
and on her wedding day
Those same old words wer
the words I had to say

Keep in touch, keep in touch
That's what we always say
when we part to go
our individual ways
keep in touch, keep in touch
please write or give me a ring
to let me know how things
are going your way
At 48 years old my sweet
wife passed away
And as she did, she put her
trembling hand in mine
Then said those words of
parting as she pointed to the sky
Keep in touch with Him
and I'll see you by and by

Keep in touch, keep in touch with Him
He's coming soon I know
We'll be together
in that mansion in the sky
Keep in touch, keep in touch with Him
I know He'll see you through
And with that she sweetly
smiled a goodbye
And now the dark clouds gathe
as the years keep slipping by
And those I've touched seem
much to busy to keep in touch

*They placed me in a home
and left me all alone
"We'll keep in touch," they said as
they headed off for home*

*Keep in touch, keep in touch
That's what we always say
when we part to go
our individual ways
keep in touch, keep in touch
please write or give me a ring
to let me know how things are going
your way*

*I long to know how things
are going your way*

It was about 10 pm when he got on the phone and called Sandra.

"It was a rough day at work. I don't know how dad did it all. Since your mom is gone and my parents as well, we might as well move in together. Would you rather live at your house or mine? Sandra thought it over for a while. She was eating an olive and mayo sandwich.

"It does not matter to me. Your place does not have a fireplace though and this one does. I really like to snuggle up in your arms on a cold night. With Christmas coming up, we can stay here at least until spring, then we can move to your house if you like. How was your day at work other than rough?"

"The team welcomed me in. That surprised me since when I tried to work there before, I was not well received. I am more mature now and they know about the baby. I can do this but am really tired out. Is it alright if I hang out here for the night then meet up with you tomorrow after work? We can come over here and load up a few things or you can drive your Ma's car over and meet me. It looks like she will not be using it again."

"Ok, I will be alright. I will lock the door and then tomorrow come over about the time you get off. By the way, what time will you get off tomorrow?"

"About five. I should be home by 5:30 unless it takes a lot to close. We are going to need some money to live on. I will see if there are some funds from the business, I can get my hands on. Then we probably need to go grocery shopping."

Even though he was tired, another song came popping into his mind and he took up the old guitar and started strumming it out with some words.

LOVE ME TODAY

Lonely, yes I was lonely.
I was a stranger to my despair
Gently you came and touched me,
tried to show me that you cared
Slowly I grew to trust you,
like a flower trust the sun
Softly our love was growing,
and now this lovely day is gone

Love me, today, just love me.
Don't let the time keep slipping by
Hold me tonight just hold me.
A love left waiting will often die
Feel me, tonight just feel me.
My heart is longing for your touch
Love me, tonight just love me,
because I love you oh so much.
Quickly, the morning's passing,
soon you'll love me yes you will
Surely by noon you'll hold me.
In your arms secure I'll feel
Ready, yes I am ready.
I hear the birds sing goodnight songs
Slowly, the daylight's fading.
I'll dream I loved you all night long

Love me, today, just love me.

Don't let the time keep slipping by
Hold me tonight just hold me.
A love left waiting will often die
Feel me, tonight just feel me.
My heart is longing for your touch
Love me, tonight just love me,
because I love you oh so much.

A couple of weeks passed and so did Christmas for this young couple. Paul had finished moving in with Sandra. They had managed to get a Christmas tree or rather a branch from a tree and scrounged around the house until they found some lights and ornaments. For dinner they ordered pizza from a parlor in town. They went together to pick it up. The money had not been as easy to come by as Paul thought. Bill still did not trust him completely because of past failings I expect. He had taken control of the business. He really, deep down inside did not want this legal owner to assert his ownership. Being a man of opportunity, he wished the lad would just go away. He had put in hours and hours to build the business up side by side with Paul's dad. Now this kid who had probably not worked a full day in his life before these last couple of weeks was coming around like he owned the place. Well, he probably did but that would change. Bill had secured a lawyer who was somewhat crooked in his dealings. He would rather shovel out a few thousand to him now than loose thousands and thousands of dollars later to the kid.

After Sandra and Paul finished eating and opening a present, the lady made a request.

"This is our first, real Christmas together. It has been quite a memorial one. Could you sing a song or something to commemorate it?" Her eyes were sparkling as she asked. Paul thought it over and decided to give it a try. He picked up his electric guitar this time, plugged it into the amp and started to think of some words. While playing he started this song out speaking.

MERRY CHRISTMAS ANYWAY

You know Christmas is that happy time of year when friends and families get together. There's the Christmas tree with its pretty ornaments and lights and then of course the presents. They look so nice all wrapped up with paper and ribbon. And just outside the window the little snowflakes sift down gently. I love a white Christmas. I always like to go Christmas shopping in the snow. The town is decorated so pretty with all the colored lights and dear old Santa, with his long white beard and red suit, is pasted on every window. I just love Christmas. Especially the Christmas dinner with the family and the faces of those little children are so happy. They get so excited when it comes time to open everything up. Their voices ring out with squeals of laughter. And in the background Christmas carols play softly while jungle bells ring. Christmas, Merry Christmas. It is such a wonderful time. But this year it rained all Christmas, and I sang:

Merry Christmas Anyway,
Merry Christmas Anyway.
The snow is bound to come someday.
We'll have a Merry, Merry Christmas anyway.

And do you know what else? I didn't even get to go Christmas shopping in the snow. And I didn't even get to buy a Christmas present for my sweetheart either. But the day before Christmas we got three bills in the mail, one for the gas, one for the water and one for the phone. But I sang:

> *Merry Christmas Anyway,*
> *Merry Christmas Anyway.*
> *Better times will come they say.*
> *We'll have a Merry Christmas Anyway.*

Most people get together with their families and friends for Christmas Dinner, but do you know what? My parents were gone to who knows where, and my sister and her family were way up north. Our closest friends were in California. My sweethearts Mom was in limbo. Her sister and their family were out east, and her brother was in Ohio. They really were. But we sang:

> *Merry Christmas Anyway,*
> *Merry Christmas Anyway.*
> *We'll all get together again someday.*
> *We'll have a Merry Christmas Anyway.*

So, my sweetheart and I spent Christmas curled up under a blanket by the fireplace watching the light blink on our Christmas tree. We only had one blinking light. The rest didn't blink. We were glad for a Christmas tree even though it was from a branch the neighbor cut off from a spruce when he did some trimming. As for the rain outside? At least it was warm under the blanket as the logs burned down to embers. We gave the kitten some cheese wrapped up in Christmas paper. She packed it all over the room shaking her little head until the paper tore off then she ate it. It was kinda cute. There were two presents under our branch and those came from my aunt. So we sang:

Merry Christmas Anyway,
Merry Christmas Anyway.
There'll be another
Christmas again someday.
We'll have a Merry Christmas Anyway.

Merry Christmas Anyway,
Merry Christmas Anyway.
Better times will come they say.
We'll have a Merry, Merry Christmas
Anyway.

Merry Christmas Anyway,
my Love. I love you.

Meanwhile in another CUBICLE of time John and Kathy went on their first date in a long time. It was the small restaurant where they first met. Kat had been a waiter there. She was young and beautiful back in those days and when this giant of six foot five inches walked in to grab a meal, their eyes had locked. Some might still believe in love at first sight. If so, this was probably just such a case. She was surprised when he left her a twenty-dollar tip. When the owner was occupied in back, she bent down and whispered in his ear.

"We are required to split up the tips between all three waiters so you should make that a little smaller and maybe we can catch up on the rest another time." John loved her frankness. He took the bill ever so softly in his large hands and replaced it with a two-dollar bill.

"What do you do with these," he smiled? "Do you cut them in half or thirds?" He winked when he mentioned thirds. She smiled her best smile and stated.

"I will get this one all for myself.

Thank you very much. But I would have preferred the twenty under different circumstances." From that meeting their love had blossomed. Now they were here again and in the background some Christmas music was playing. When a peppy song came on, they got up and danced along with two other couples. Tomorrow would be Christmas and the whole family would be together again if they could somehow persuade Paul to join them and maybe Kathy's brother and his family? The tree was all decorated and there were lots of presents waiting to be opened. But tonight? Tonight, would be wonderful! John thought of the song Paul had sung the other night. Never again would he need to love Kathy while she was sleeping. A poem started to form in his own head as they twirled there together in the light of the Christmas tree.

So put your hand in mine.
Your trembling heart will find in me
a man that's kind
Just trust your life with mine.
I know in time we'll find a love that
binds
Your body next to mine.
Try to forget the times you cried alone
So keep your hand in mine. Your

trembling heart will find a home

He would run it by Paul next time he was over. Perhaps between the two of them they could come up with a good one.

CHAPTER FOUR

The Symbiotron rechecked the monitors. Something was going haywire in sector eight. He removed three of his compound eyes from other monitors and zeroed them in on an elderly gentleman. In the real world he would be having a heart attack. In his CUBE, he was also. But the CUBE was supposed to have a life support system that did not allow that to happen. If these humans had any medical problems happen to them physically, the slime-matter was supposed to detect it and prevent it from happening. Sector eight was easy enough to get to. He could be there in less than two minutes, by the human time clock. He flipped a few levers with some of his appendages and set the system on autopilot. He stopped in front of the CUBE of Joe Marlo. Focusing seven of his compound eyes gave him x-ray vision. He penetrated the layers of the old man's body one at a time until his heart was exposed. It was then he saw the pacemaker. Joe did not need it now. That was in fact what was causing all the problems. His upper, left appendage passed through the outer protection shield as if it were not even there and into the man's heart. With two little pinchers he removed the pacemaker and the tiny electrical circuitry as skillfully as any heart surgeon. The seizures of the old man stopped and the look of terror on his face abated. In short order he was in bed resting, at least in his mind. His deceased wife was there beside him. For a while he had been running a fever. Now as his head cooled, he spoke. The insectoid did not hang around to listen.

What started out to be a controlled environment to observe and play around with the genes of arthropods had backfired. There had been enough progress made to create human sized insects from a lab that first originated in France. Later it was moved underground. The Insect branch of the arthropods were ugly things when increased to the size of a person. When the developer of this technology suddenly died in the lab, one of the students had quickly placed him in a (RNAi CRISPR-Cas9) chamber. He had been kept alive for weeks. Finally, when his time ran out, this student had transferred his brain into the head of an insect. Since life forms seldom died in these controlled environments, the transplanted brain adapted itself to its new host. There were several advantages to being an insect. The strong exoskeleton at this size were nearly indestructible. The multiple eyes and appendages were great for multitasking. And so, the Symbiotron had risen to superior powers. Eventually after escaping from his confinement, he had killed all the lab assistants. He had also created gene manipulated creatures like himself by transplanting the brains of these people into this new species. Now there were dozens of them, and the number was growing because they discovered they could multiply by natural means. He stopped by the nursery on his way back to the controls. There were millions and millions of eggs laid. There were also lots of larvae in different states of growth. Within a matter of days there would be an innumerable number of them.

There had been a problem with the new ones though. There were not enough human brains to go around so Zeddafina, the father Symbiotron had figured out a way to place humans in the observation chambers so they could be controlled and experimented on. There was a small processor in their brain that could be paired with the brains of the insectoids. In this way they could function without the transplant itself. When a person was CUBED, there needed to be at least one arthropod captured with them. It could be an insect, a spider or any of the other creatures that fell under this category. There were some arthropod properties that enabled them to see in all directions at the same time. Zed, with the help of the arthropods from the world of humans, could see multiple things happening at the same time. He had linked up millions and millions of these creatures in a universal hive mind. This worked wonderfully. The more insects that were hooked into the mind, the greater was their ability to see all and be omnipresent up there you might say. Zeddafina's mind had grown larger than life. He now operated from billions of locations all over the earth. As for the structures, there were certain chemicals insects released to form substances that prolonged their life and made their exoskeletons harder than steel at these enlarged sizes. He had added a formula to make that substance into transparent chambers. Using the technology of the bees, he had created the chambers. These were square though and not hexagonal. Millions of them stood ready to be filled. And so, the entire nightmare had begun. Humans were now the ones in control chambers and the master mind of the hive mind headed all of it up.

The liquid within the chambers enabled the subconscious and the conscious mind of the humans to become one. Those things that had been recorded in their subconscious mind blended with their conscious mind. The memories of people who had died or stepped out of the lives of their associates were as real in the subconscious as they had been in real life. That is how people who had been out of reality could reassert themselves into this new, virtual reality so readily. If a person had a memory of someone else at the subconscious level, they still existed. When a person was in a relationship with another, all five of their senses had been involved in recording each encounter in endless tracks of the subconscious. As the upper and lower minds were united, the senses all worked to make them as real to the person as they had ever been, even down to the smallest detail. Certain properties of the arthropods added greater reality to the environment. The people in the chambers were living a life that was as real or even more so than those outside who had not been encased in this all-sustaining liquid environment. There is also a property of many arthropods that enables them to go into hibernation as colder temperatures come. This chemical reaction was present in the chambers. The hibernation effect slowed down the physical properties of the humans to the point where they needed far less nutrition to sustain their life. Heart rates were so low, if this were to happen in the open air, people would die. There was no need for liquids because they were in a liquid. Since their bodily organs were operating so minimally, the natural waste excretions that humans have from day to day were also greatly minimized. If this technology were made available to humanity today, millions of lives could be prolonged.

Imagine taking a trip to a distant star or galaxy. In this type of suspended animation, humans could travel for decades. When they emerged, they would be as young as they were ten or twenty years ago. During that time, the hive mind of the entire race would keep churning out new experiences. If a human wished to learn some new skill or course of study while traveling, they could have this programed into the solution they were immersed in and upon exiting would have that knowledge in-brained within. It really was a clever invention. So far it was turning out to be a great enterprise. Half of humanity was finally happy. Zed had done what no other entity had accomplished. That was to solve nearly all the ills and problems of humanity. The insectoids that were now in control of much of the planet were a peaceful race of creatures. They avoided conflict. They co-operated with one another. They shared a portion of each other's mind so problems could be quickly solved and eliminated. They also had big dreams and loved to be contented. These traits spilled over into their human subjects.

The vice president of the United States of America sat in the oval office wondering what course to pursue. She had been sworn into the office of President at his parting. Now as the realization of the thousands of decisions she needed to make dawned upon her, she was overwhelmed with the task. The Department of Security had all the stops pulled. There was one and only one task, find out what was behind the CUBE and eliminate the threat. Had not all the troublemakers been mysteriously taken into CUBES themselves, there would have been far more problems. Whoever was behind this loved peace and not war. She decided to call a meeting with the Department of Defense and get them together with some of the top brass of the Department of Security to see if there had been any uptick in UFO or extraterrestrial activity. Was an alien race with superior technology and strategy behind this whole phenomenon? She arranged for a meeting with them in the morning at 10 am sharp. If any of them were even a minute late, they would be locked out. She had made this plain after taking office. Business was business and every minute was important. If a person could not make an appointment on time, there was no appointment for them.

When the hour arrived the next day, everyone that had been contacted was present and accounted for. Each of them had lost family members to the CUBE. They all had seen these structures rise out of the ground and capture their victims then disappear after a few hours or of late a few minutes. This had to stop. The entire age of the population was under sixty. There was not an elderly person out there so far as was known. A few hundred thousand nursing homes had closed, and hospitals were inactive as accidents were not allowed to happen and when one was about to, the CUBES would rise out of the ground and prevent them before they took place. Unfortunately, that always meant less people would be left to do what needed to be done. A population of nearly four-hundred thousand had been reduced to around a hundred-sixty thousand. Immigrants were not coming into the country anymore either because the people that had overseen their nations had all succumbed to the CUBE. The multiple communist's parties had melted away and democracy was the main form of government world-wide. Somehow the spirit of the peace-loving race behind this all had spilled over to the remaining living. People cooperated with each other now rather than engage in fighting for power. In many ways the world was much better.

Behind it all, Zeddafina was really a genius although those gathered in the room did not know of him yet. Would they ever? What if they did? Was the world not better off with half of its population missing in action? Where in the name of science had they vanished to? Could science even figure it all out? After the call to order, Roger started out.

"I have heard reports that the CUBE will not form around them if the person being targeted cries out a series of three nos. All they have to utter before being succumbed is 'No. No. No.' It has worked in hundreds of cases worldwide. If this information can get out to the public, we can save a lot of lives." Theodore spoke next

.

"What Roger just stated is true. It happened to me. I was about to be sideswiped from an out of control, on-coming vehicle when I cried out, 'No. No. No.' The person in the other car did not say that and was taken. I am amazed at how the time frame has lessened. The CUBES used to be visible for hours, then they went down to minutes, now they appear to be coming in seconds. Whatever is behind this is gaining more intelligence with each passing day. I wonder if its intent is to take us all?" The president spoke up next.

"You stated that as if you believe there is one mastermind in control of all the CUBES. Could there not be a lot more than one?"

"There might be but this, I feel, they have in common. There is something controlling the entire process. I used to work with bees. Among them there was something we called the hive mind. One entity controlled the whole so they all could work together in teamwork. I believe this is the same thing we are witnessing today. There is a universal or mastermind behind it all, uniting millions and millions of minds, linking them together for some purpose nobody understands." Greg spoke up next. He was a little short guy with thick glasses. They had dropped down on his nose and he pushed them up before asking his question.

"Have we seen any increase in UFO activity of late? Are the sightings up or down? If we can answer this, we may be able to determine if some alien force is behind all of it. It is rumored many of those races have superior mental ability than humans even to the point of a universal mind or telepathy." Roger answered the question.

"There has been a downturn of sightings. They are about half as frequent as they were before this all started. Of course, that could be because we have half the population, we once had so the sheer numbers of missing persons could be the cause of that and not the lack of extraterrestrial activity. People are also avoiding running around in the dark as much as they used to do since more than half of the captures have happened after dark. Whatever it is, light or darkness make no difference to it. It must have night vision capabilities." The meeting lasted for exactly an hour. True to her form the President brought it to an end to cover another appointment she had set up for a quarter after eleven. It was hard to say if any problems were solved. I guess there was one. If a person wanted to disappear into the mist, just keep silent. For the rest of the nation the message must go out. "Speak 'No. No. No.' now or forever hold your peace.

One day, one of the CUBED persons returned from the cosmos. He made national news. Millions of people all over the country heard his testimony. Though he did not say how he came back, he did express a desire to go back. He said the world in the CUBE was paradise on earth. Nothing ever went wrong in there. People who had died were united with their families. Problems that had illuded being solved were fixed in that place, wherever it was. He, spoke of his mother and father getting back together after a long, nasty divorce. His little sister that had terminal cancer was completely healed and running around like any normal child. He, spoke of the gatherings of families and friends that always brought surprises as a person they had not heard from in years might suddenly show. Where he had come from, the world was lush and green. There was no air pollution. Crime was non-existent. You could not ask for a better world. Everyone appeared to be happy. When they asked him who was president of the United States he stated.

"You know him. He has been in office all this time and done wonders. He has arranged world peace with all the nations. Wars have stopped and the economy is booming." When they told them in this world the president had disappeared, he could not believe it.

"Who then is president, now?"

"The Vice-President of course. She is beside herself and does not know what to do to stop all the people from getting transferred away to never, never land."

"Why would she want to stop it? It is paradise where I came from." As millions and millions of people were watching on television screens all over, the CUBE came and whisked him away. After that a lot of people were less frightened about going if their time to go came. Others who were hurting from losses of close family members or friends went out and tried to arrange for accidents or commit crimes so the CUBE would come and take them away to paradise. Another fifth of the population of the US were gone a month later.

Zeddafina was rather pleased with the propaganda that he had managed to get across to the world. The more people he controlled, the more power he had. The world was now his for the taking. He determined to not quit until every man, woman, child and other were within the confines of his chambers.

Back at the ranch no more cattle had been scooped away. The herd was increasing in size again and the three remaining children were hanging out together, some with new partners. Life was not so bad now, really. Humanity still experienced loss. It was not called death though for if a person was about to die, a CUBE seemed to anticipate it and arrive in time to capture its victim while they were still breathing. Who knew what happened to them once the CUBE vanished? They had all heard the testimony of David. Since then, there had been others who returned for a moment or two to encourage others to go to the land of promise before it was too late. As more and more of them came back, their effect became less and less enticing. People choose to live with the known rather than risk the unknown world of the CUBE. Being stripped of all your clothing and floating around in a liquid environment was not their idea of paradise.

With the decrease in population

worldwide, there was far less pollution. The great forest fires that had ravaged the nation for so many years ceased to happen. If a fire got out of control, a cold wind would rise out of the earth and stop it before it had a chance to spread. If a person were caught in that chill, they were captured unless they cried out "No. No. No." Perhaps the CUBE would have been humanities destiny had not a new order of being emerged in the underground labs of the Symbiotron.

CHAPTER FIVE

A mutation occurred in one of the incubation chambers. The new creature appeared to show qualities of intelligence far to soon. He also had a golden color to his body that made him beautiful if insectoids can be called beautiful. The team monitored his growth carefully. They took samples of his genes and in short order were able, with the RNAi CRISPR, to bring into existence an assortment of colors to the newbies. Even the older ones edited their makeup to take on some colors. What they did not realize though was every time a little fragment of Zylonelder entered their biological make up, so did a piece of the mind of the originator. He did not appreciate being a peacemaker. He loved causing trouble. As he grew, so did his self-importance. It did not happen immediately, but Zeddafina noticed changes in his billions of captives. They became less and less cooperative and more and more agitated. The relations between the humans started breaking up. Zylonelder allowed his mind to expand more and more. After he noticed that Zeddafina noticed, he backed off his influence for a while so that the old one could go back into his power-trance. Then within a matter of twenty-four human hours, the newcomer struck with force. Things went wild in the land of the CUBED. The universal hive-mind was segmented. That overriding element of peace and tranquility vanished.

When John came home with flowers for Kathy one evening, she met him at the door with a photo she had found. It was a picture of John with his arm around Amy, his secretary. Normally this would not have raised any suspicion, but she had seen her husband at a restaurant with another woman a day earlier when she went in for some groceries. She could not see the face of the gal, but she had dark, brown hair and in the photo, Amy had very dark, brown hair. John was given a blanket and asked to sleep on the couch. He tried to explain that it was not Amy at all but a visiting saleswoman who had just given him his largest order to date. He was going to surprise Kathy with a nice trip to the Caribbean once the paperwork was completed and the goods exchanged for payment.

Paul experienced a similar event when he returned late from the tire business one evening. Sandra was crying when he came home. Little Lesa was on death's doorstep. Her fever was at 106 degrees. If they could not get it down soon, she would suffer permanent brain damage. Sandra blew up and blamed Paul for it all as Bill and his father had not completed the paperwork for their medical expenses. There was not enough money in their combine accounts to pay the bill that was sure to arrive a few weeks after the little girl went to the hospital. This went on for weeks even after the fever was down and Lisa recovered. What used to be like coming home to heaven was now like coming home to hell. True to his nature, Paul went to the old guitar and took out his frustration in a song. He did not do it at her and her mother's place but went back to his own. Mom and Dad had gone on another vacation, so he had the house all to himself. The words started out slowly at first but then gathered momentum as he started closing in on the end. By the time he was finished, he had made up his mind. He would sell what he could from his stash of things at a pawn shop and hit the road with a motor bike of some sort. It probably would not be a new one but who cared?

LEARNING TO LOVE YOU

Existence was so boring,
I started looking about
Looked in all the papers,
decided to move out
Sold my things at a pawn shop
bought me a motor bike
Hit that lonesome highway,
looking for some light

Then someone said, you were around,
That you were out of sight,
that you had some light
So now I'm learning,
learning about you
Learning about you, learning to know
you,
learning to love you

We both got on my motor,
headed for the sea
Twas a misty twilight,
a time for you and me
On that sandy shoreline,
with wave spray in the air
We lived the light together,
just happy to be there

Yes, someone said,
you were around
That you were out of sight,
that you had some light
So now I'm learning,
learning about you
Learning about you,
learning to know you,
learning to love you

Back in somewhere village,
the paper had a note
They said I was a driften,
said there was no hope
But here in love this morning,
I know that they are wrong
If love ain't in your city,
its best to move along

Yes, someone said,
you were around
That you were out of sight,
that you had some light
So now I'm learning,
learning about you
Learning about you,
learning to know you,
learning to love you

Back at the ranch, granddad had a heart attack and died right there in front of grandmother. This was not supposed to be happening. For nearly a year life had been like living in paradise. We had family reunions like people used to have in the old days before a virus broke up the nation. There were get togethers in town where all the people would come bringing goodies. There was always a live band and dancing. We would engage in games like they used to do at the country fairs. And people would show up to church. The sheriff was the face of the law but for nearly a year there had not been one major crime that caused him to open a prison cell. But now that was all changing. A murder took place on the corner of Broadway and Fifth. Christel's polio came back, and they had to pack her up and send her back to her aunt. Jake's wife of just a few months got homesick and left. Even Junior and his family had a falling out with the rest of the household and promised to never set foot in the old ranch home again. All over the globe the world of the CUBE was falling apart. Zeddafina never suspected the young, bright, intelligent, and handsome Zylonelder was behind it all. Then one day it all collapsed. People that had been gone for over a year, started popping back into existence as the structures of the CUBE failed. Humanity started to get back to normal as the dream turned nightmare broke into reality. Even the president of the United States appeared suddenly one day back in the Lincoln room as if he had never left. This caused some rather uncomfortable circumstances since the vice-president and her family had taken up habitation there. There were also some other conflicts since once having obtained to office of POTUS, she now would be required to go back to being much less in the public eye.

Coming back from church one day, back when the world was normal again and the entire CUBE system had been dismantled, Paul came up with another song. He had the experiences of both worlds in his head now, the world of the CUBE and the world of reality. I suppose you can say he was wiser for it all. At least he believed fully in God now. That was a plus. He strummed out one final song for the record as the sun set in the west. Little Lesa was there with her bright, blue eyes looking and listening as he sang away. Sandra came and sat beside him close but far enough away so it would not effect, his playing.

AND I SEE JESUS

Heaven's sure a wonder,
I can't believe my eyes
And the Tree of Life's much larger,
than I had ever realized
And the golden fruit that hangs there,
is a wonderful surprise
You can feel life flowing through you,
for in heaven no one dies

And I see Jesus, He's the one for me
Yes, I see Jesus, He set me free
O blessed Savior He came for me
I'll be with Jesus through eternity

Now the streets of gold are purer,
than any gold that we can see
And the gates of pearl are open,
that's the way John said they'd be
And I see that dazzling city,
and there's a mansion there for me
It is just beyond the river,
next to the crystal sea

And I see Jesus, see His lovely face
Yes, I see Jesus, He took my place
O blessed Savior He came for me

Now I'm with Jesus, through eternity

But just then the bright scenes all faded. And the Tree of Life was gone. And those golden streets that had sparkled, now faded from my sight. In desperation I tried to catch one last glimpse of that beautiful mansion, but it too was gone. All I could see was darkness. It was darker than I had ever know, so dark I could feel it. Then I knew that never again would this old, world hold anything for me. There was a better land, a lovely one who's builder and maker was God. I knew then that I must have my family with me. For how could I enjoy the bliss of that wonderful place knowing that somewhere in the darkness, one of them had been lost? And my friends, they too must be ready for Him to come just as He promised.

And I'll see Jesus, see His lovely face
Yes, I'll see Jesus, He took my place
O blessed Savior He came for me
I'll be with Jesus, through eternity

And we'll see Jesus, see
His lovely faceYes,we'll see Jesus,
He took our place O blessed
Savior our sins erased

We'll be with Jesus, amazing grace

Where did the idea of paradise come from? The main source I know of is in that ancient book, the Bible. In Revelation of that book a paradise to come is described in detail. It is a real place. John an apostle of Jesus was given a vision of it. If you choose to believe it, this paradise to come will not be in some virtual reality environment that encompasses all your physical senses. You will not find it at the end of some goggles or even in a cube that surrounds you with a liquid environment as in the story above. Thousands of people have come to believe in this paradise to come. It gives humanity great hope that there is more than we see and experience around us now. In the coming paradise, loved ones who have passed on will be united with us again. There will be a grand reunion in heaven.

Perhaps some of you are caught up in a false reality, a virtual one. You put those goggles on or connect some wires up to your head and are taken off into a land that is beyond your wildest imagination. It consumes your whole being. Within a matter of minutes, you are fully emersed in its reality. If so? You reader, listener, are in a CUBE. You have turned your life, your will your actions, your mind over to another entity. So long as you are within its grasp, you will be influenced by it and consumed. Your thoughts and actions will be blended with whatever its creator has made. You feel the rush as you pit your skills against creatures of all kinds, shapes and sizes. You are not only in the game, you are the game.

WAKE UP!   WAKE UP!

SPEAK NOW OR FOREVER HOLD YOUR PEACE. THREE WORDS ARE ALL YOU NEED TO SPEAK TO BREAK OUT OF THIS MIND CONTROL

NO! NO! NO!

Speak N.O.w or Forever Hold Your Peace

9 781965 126387